SCHOOL LIE

3 0 MAY 2014

BOOK NO.

CLASS

For Tom, Becca and Chris – B.M.

Text copyright © Barbara Mitchelhill 2000
Illustrations copyright © Stephen Player 2000

Published in Great Britain in 2000
by Hodder Wayland, an imprint of
Hodder Children's Books

A Catalogue record for this book is available from
British Library.

ISBN: 0 7500 2850 5

Printed in Hong Kong by Wing King Tong

Hodder Children's Books
A division of Hodder Headline
338 Euston Road, London NW1 3BH

Barbara Mitchelhill

Terror in the Attic

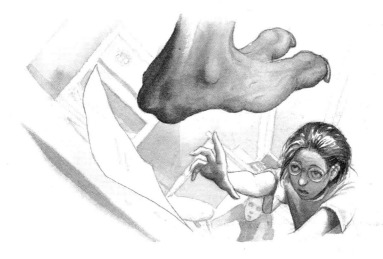

Illustrated by Stephen Player

HODDER
Wayland

an imprint of Hodder Children's Books

Chapter One

The sunshine vanished when Dorian O'Dedra arrived. Black clouds covered the sky. Even the wind wailed and blew through the smallest cracks, rattling the window frames.

He was tall and dressed in black. His face was long with eyes set so deep that they were lost in the shadow of his forehead.

"Who is he?" Craig asked his sister, Kelly.

"The new lodger," said Kelly, pressing her nose to the window. "He's gruesome!"

Tracy squeezed between them to get a better view as he raised his hand to lift the knocker.

Three knocks echoed down the hall, *bang,*
bang, bang, and Mum hurried to the door.

Close up, he was even stranger, giving off a
heavy, sweet, sickly smell which made them
hold their breath and wrinkle their noses.

Mum introduced them. "These are my children, Craig and Kelly," she said. "And this is their friend, Tracy, who lives next door."

Dorian O'Dedra said nothing. Not a word. He simply frowned disapprovingly.

"Mr O'Dedra is a writer," Mum said. "He's here to do some research."

They tried to chat politely. They even offered to carry his luggage upstairs. But he shook his head and stepped back, clutching a black bag as if it contained the Crown Jewels.

"Weird!" said Craig, after he had disappeared upstairs. "And what's in that bag of his?"

Tracy grinned. "That's what I'd like to know."

Just for a laugh, they agreed to sneak into the attic bedroom the next day and find the answer.

Chapter Two

The next morning, Dorian O'Dedra left early and Mum decided to do some gardening.

"We'd like to help," Kelly lied, "but we've got a project to do before we go back to school."

Mum was impressed. "I'm glad you're taking your schoolwork seriously." With that, she pulled on her gardening gloves and walked out through the back door.

"Let's go up now," said Craig. "We won't wait for Tracy."

Tingling with excitement, they took the spare key from the bunch by the door.

"We'll stay half an hour, that's all," said Kelly. "We daren't let Mum catch us. She'll go crazy."

Up in the attic bedroom the window was wide open and the curtains were blowing in the breeze. Even so, the room was filled with the sickly-sweet smell they had noticed yesterday.

Kelly crossed to the window and leaned out. "Hey! Come and look!" she said. In the old graveyard next to the house, among the crumbling headstones, stood Dorian O'Dedra, his black coat flapping crazily in the wind.

"What's he doing?" asked Craig.

Kelly shrugged her shoulders. "Talking to the dead, I should think. Who cares? Let's look for that bag."

They found the leather bag on the floor by the bed. "Nothing!" said Craig as he peered inside. "It's empty!"

In fact, the only things they could see that belonged to Dorian O'Dedra were a pile of plain paper and an old typewriter set on the desk.

"Only somebody who's really weird would bring a thing like that," said Kelly. "Most people have laptops."

"Come on," said Craig. "This is boring. Let's go downstairs and watch TV."

But as they turned to go, they heard *tap... tap... tap...*

They spun round and stared. The typewriter was slowly typing a message. They leaned closer to read it.

WHAT DO YOU WANT?

"Wow!" said Kelly. "Not so boring! A trick
typewriter! No wonder he didn't want us to
carry it."

"Yeah," said Craig, bending over it. "Now
that's cool! I wonder what happens when
you type a reply."

"Let me!" said Kelly, pushing him aside.

Giggling, she placed her fingers on the
keys. Suddenly they felt icy cold and a shiver
rippled down her spine.

"Go on!" insisted Craig. "Type something."

So Kelly tapped out:

I WANT TWO TICKETS FOR THE BEAT BAND CONCERT ON FRIDAY.

Craig groaned. "Pathetic! Where's your imagination?"

"What would you have said?" snapped Kelly.

"I don't know..."

They were interrupted by a noise downstairs in the hall. They stood stock still and listened. Someone was opening the front door.

Kelly raced across to the window. "I can't see him!" she said. "He must be coming back. He'll catch us red-handed!"

Chapter Three

Dorian O'Dedra had not returned. The noise they had heard was an envelope being pushed through the letter box.

They went downstairs and picked it up off the mat. "It's got my name on it!" said Kelly and tore it open. "Wow! Two tickets for the Beat Band Concert! Mum said she'd try to get some. Brilliant!" She grinned at her brother. "I've got to tell Tracy."

As Kelly turned and reached for the
phone, Craig headed upstairs. He had to try
out the typewriter for himself...

From the attic-room window, he could see
Dorian O'Dedra was back in the graveyard,
standing still like a great black crow. He
seemed to be talking to someone, or
something, muttering under his breath and
waving his arms. It was spooky!

Craig walked over to the typewriter. He leaned over and stared as the keys typed *tap... tap... tap...*

WHAT DO YOU WANT?

Was it a trick typewriter? he wondered. Or was it something supernatural? He knew he had to try it or he would never know.

He placed his fingers on the keys. Suddenly they felt icy cold and a shiver rippled down his spine. Craig paused, shrugged it off and quickly tapped out:

I WANT TO FLY.

Chapter Four

Kelly put the phone down. It was engaged –
Tracy's mum talking again! She turned to
speak to Craig but he had gone.

She raced up the stairs shouting, "Craig!
Why didn't you wait for me?" She flung
open the door of the attic bedroom and
looked inside but Craig wasn't there. The
room was empty... except for a large black
bat hanging from the ceiling.

"Aggghhh!" Kelly screamed and pressed her back to the wall. The bat swooped and she yelled, covering her face. Again and again it swooped. "Get lost!" she shouted in desperation and grabbed Dorian O'Dedra's leather bag and flung it at the creature.

It missed. The bat dived at her. Again she threw the bag and this time it struck the bat and knocked it to the floor.

Nervously, she stepped over to the black shape. Was it dead? No. It twitched. She could see its pulse beating through the hairy skin. Then, to her horror, she saw fangs protruding from its open mouth.

"A vampire bat!" she said and shivered. "You're not having my blood!"

She grabbed a heavy brass lamp off the chest of drawers and raised it above her head, ready to strike.

Chapter Five

She was about to smash the bat with the lamp when she heard a thin, reedy voice.

"Don't do it, Kelly!"

She let her arms drop to her side.

"It's me. Craig."

Kelly's mouth fell open.

"Look at the typewriter," he squeaked.

Kelly hurried over to the machine and saw the words I WANT TO FLY typed on the paper.

In that moment, she realized the typewriter had sent those tickets – not Mum. And now it had turned Craig into a bat.

Kelly groaned "So what do we do?"

"I don't know," he sobbed. "I wish I'd never touched that typewriter."

Kelly was pacing backwards and forwards around the room.

"There's only one thing I can think of," she said, "and I don't know if it will work."

"Please try it, Kelly. *Please*!"

She took a deep breath and nodded. "I'll be back in two secs," she said and raced downstairs to the kitchen.

Grabbing the box of matches from the cupboard, Kelly ran back to the attic. Then with shaking hands, she struck a match, pulled the paper from the typewriter and held it to the flame.

Her heart was racing. If her plan didn't work, Craig could be trapped forever inside the body of a bat.

Chapter Six

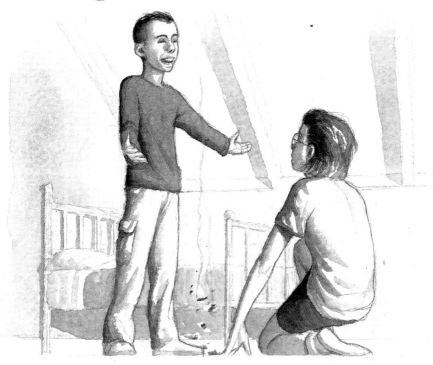

Before the ashes of the paper fell to the floor, Craig was back to his old self.

"Wow! It worked!" he yelled. "You're brilliant, sis!"

Kelly was furious. "We shouldn't have come up here. Mr O'Dedra could be back any minute!"

But Craig didn't see it that way. He was too excited.

"This typewriter is awesome!" he said. "It must be supernatural." He stood near it and rubbed his hands. "Just think! We can do anything we want and, if things go wrong, we just destroy the paper. Easy!"

He placed another sheet into the typewriter.

"Don't, Craig!" yelled Kelly. But before she could say anything else, the keys began to tap out the words:

WHAT DO YOU WANT?

"Leave it!" she shouted. "Don't touch it!"

Craig grinned. "Cool it, sis!" he said. "I'll ask to be a brilliant footballer – what can go wrong?"

Kelly was hysterical. "No!" she screamed, but Craig had already typed:

I WANT TO BE A—

Then the door burst open.

"Hey! I've been knocking on the back door for five minutes." It was Tracy. "What's that?" she said, pointing at the typewriter.

"A supernatural typewriter," said Craig.

"Oh yeah! Let's have a go." And she pushed him out of the way and read what he had typed. "I'll finish it for you."

"Don't touch it," yelled Kelly.

But it was too late. She had already typed MONSTER and was doubled up laughing. "You're a monster already, Craig!"

Nothing happened for a minute or so. Kelly and Craig waited, holding their breath, their eyes fixed on Tracy. Then she began to change. First her skin turned green and scaly, then lumps appeared and she began to swell.

"W-what's happening?" she moaned.

Craig and Kelly watched in horror. Tracy had reached the ceiling. Black hairs sprouted as her arms grew. Then her hands grew claws as long and sharp as knitting needles. Last of all, her voice disappeared and she let out an almighty, deafening roar.

Chapter Seven

The monster rampaged around the room. Nothing was safe. Soon the bed was torn apart. The mirror was shattered. The window was smashed. Terrified, Craig and Kelly crouched in the corner.

"We've got to get the paper and burn it!" said Kelly. "It's the only way to stop that monster!"

"I'll try," said Craig.

When the monster's back was turned, he crept to the desk and slid beneath it. Just in time! The monster spun round, grabbing a small chair and flinging it furiously across the room. *Crash!*

Slowly, Craig's head appeared from under the desk top. Then his arm reached towards the typewriter... His fingers felt for the paper... But – oh no! – a gust of wind ripped though the broken window. It caught the paper and sent it flapping to the floor.

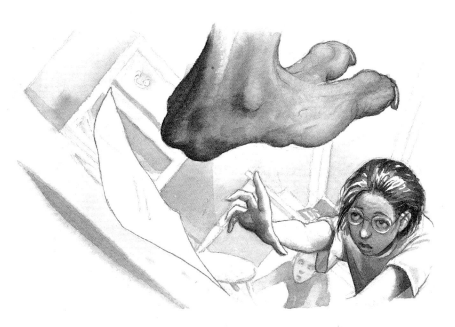

Kelly watched, horrified. She knew she had to help. She lunged forward and tried to grab the paper. But it fluttered further away and stopped at the monster's feet. It was too late! The creature grasped the paper, stuffed it in its mouth and swallowed it whole. Now it was gone for ever!

Desperate to hide, Kelly raced across the room to join Craig. But the monster saw. With a deafening roar, it charged towards the desk, breathing tongues of flames. The heat was unbearable.

"We'll fry!" said Craig.

"Or be r-ripped apart," Kelly stammered.

That was when the door was flung open and they saw the looming shape of Dorian O'Dedra, his face black as thunder.

Craig and Kelly clung together as they watched him lift his arm and point at the monster. Their hearts pounded as the monster stopped… shuddered… and froze.

"O'Dedra's hands!" whispered Craig. "Look!"

They were covered in black hairs and his bony fingers were tipped with nails as long and sharp as knitting needles.

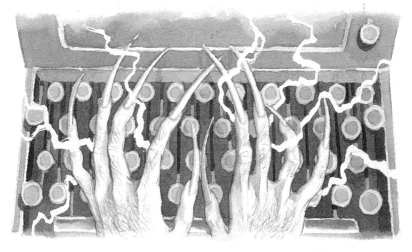

They watched him walk towards the desk and lean over the typewriter. Did he know they were there? They didn't think so. He placed his fingers on the keys and typed until sparks flew and whizzed around the room, filling it with a light so dazzling that Craig and Kelly shut their eyes and covered them with their hands.

Then Dorian O'Dedra began to speak and they knew for sure he had seen them.

"You dared to meddle with the machine," he said. "Your meddling has ruined my life's work. You will be punished."

They tried to open their eyes – but they couldn't. Suddenly, a sweet, sickly smell rose through their nostrils and filled their heads. They felt dizzy. They were falling… falling… falling… into a deep, black pit.

Chapter Eight

They woke to the sound of Mum's voice. "Come down, it's time for lunch."

The three children blinked and looked around the attic bedroom. There was no sign of Dorian O'Dedra. No monster. No broken window. No smashed furniture. The typewriter had gone, too. There was no sign of anything that had happened that morning.

They scrambled to their feet and hurried out of the door, locking it behind them.

"Coming, Mum!" Kelly shouted as they ran downstairs. "We've been studying in my bedroom."

Mum looked up as they walked into the kitchen. "Studying?" she said. "I don't think so! Look at you! Go and wash that silly stuff off your hands!"

They looked down and gasped. Black hairs had sprouted on the backs and their nails were as long and sharp as knitting needles.

In a panic, they raced up to the bathroom. They reached for the scissors and a pumice stone. They snipped at their horny nails until they were short. They scoured the backs of their hands until they were smooth and painfully raw but hairless.

But was that the end of it?

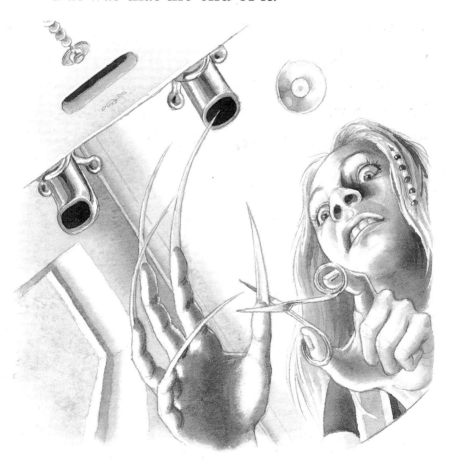

From that day on, no one saw Dorian O'Dedra. Mum never mentioned the lodger who only stayed one night. But the children knew he hadn't really left. The sweet, sickly smell lingered on and new lodgers refused the attic room.

Worse still, on wild and stormy nights, the children would hear the typewriter *tap...*

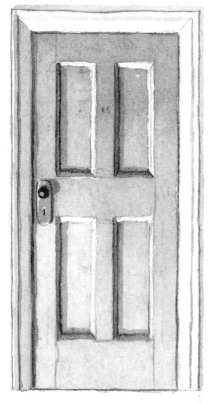

tap... tap... If they were tempted to look inside the room – if they opened the door even a crack – they knew what would happen. Black hairs would sprout on their hands, their nails would grow long and sharp – just as a warning. Just in case they dared to meddle again...

DARE TO BE SCARED!

*Are you brave enough to try more titles in the Tremors
series? They're guaranteed to chill your spine...*

Beware the Wicked Web by Anthony Masters
In the dead of night, Rob and Sam explore the forbidden
attic at the top of their new home. When they find a
sprawling, sticky web, with a giant egg at its centre, they
are scared – but not nearly as scared as when they discover
that the egg is just about to hatch...

Play... if you dare by Ruth Symes
Josie can't believe her luck when she finds the computer
game at a car boot sale. "Play... if you dare," the game
challenges her – and she does. Each level of the game
is scarier than the last. When she reaches the final level
she knows that if she dares to play on she could be
trapped for ever...

The Root of Evil by Barbara Mitchelhill
When Jake, Amy and Wez find the old pocket watch, they
are thrilled. "We'll sell it!" says Jake. After all, finders are
keepers, aren't they? So they sell the watch and go on
a wild spending spree. But then things go horribly and
frighteningly wrong...

*All these books and many more can be purchased from your
local bookseller. For more information about Tremors, write to:
The Sales Department, Hodder Children's Books,
338 Euston Road, London, NW1 3BH.*